THE FLOATING SHRINE

VOLUME - 1

DEVANSH RAJ

INDIA · SINGAPORE · MALAYSIA

ISBN 979-8-89588-963-3

CONTENTS

Contents

CHAPTER 1

PLANS

"I am so bored!!!" Anshuman grumbled, munching on a chocolate bar while leaning against the balcony railing. Preeti, his sister, glanced up from her painting, frowning.

"I know, right?! The holidays feel so far away this term. Assignments and finals are draining my soul!" She sighed, digging through a sea of stationery in search of the perfect shade of purple.

"Look who's talking! You'll probably score the highest in your whole class again, while I'm certain I'll fail Math. You know how terrible I am at tables." The eight-year-old boy gazed down sadly.

"Don't worry; we still have more than a month left for finals. I'll help you if you struggle at any point." she said, leaning closer to her canvas. "Besides, I can't wait for this term to end so we can hang out with the rest of the gang and plan for the summer."

Anshu sighed. "Yeah, the good ol' Six, back together again. We have so much fun! Remember last time when we raised money to help people affected by floods in Kerala? We collected so much! It must've been around a million, don't you think?"

Preeti raised an eyebrow. "And you still wonder why you're bad at Math."

Her brother grinned foolishly.

Anshuman and Preeti lived in Bangalore with their parents, Jatin and Parineeti. Jatin ran a chain of schools across the state, while Parineeti was the proud owner of a successful boutique. Hence, the siblings enjoyed all the best care and amenities as kids.

Anshu looked out over the balcony. "I think I want something different this holiday. Something out of the box." he mused.

"And how do you plan on making that happen?" Preeti panted, tired from painting all morning.

"Well, I'm not saying we need to go somewhere like we always do; instead, we could just stay here and find something fun to do." Anshu replied, furrowing his brow.

Preeti laughed. "You and your fantasies! As if Mom and Dad will let you stay after what happened last time."

"Hey, that vase was right in the way of the ball! Otherwise, everything would've been fine." Anshu protested.

"Who told you to turn the living room into a cricket pitch? You sent glass flying to every corner of the house! We had to tiptoe around for a week to avoid getting hurt." Preeti said, arms crossed and brow raised.

Then she fell into thought for a moment. "To be honest, I wouldn't mind staying put for once. I get it, it's kind of boring always going somewhere with our family at the start of the holidays. It's loads of fun, but it's sort of become a tradition."

"I know, right? Plus, the gang hasn't been able to meet up much during holiday time because of this. We go off, then Nishu and Aaru jet off somewhere, then El, and then Rosh. Before we know it, school reopens, and we're only meeting on weekends or at society functions."

Their four friends—Nishan, Arya, Elena, and Roshan— lived in the same apartment complex. They were very close and often gathered to play and have fun.

Both siblings sat in silence for a moment, pondering the situation. Then Preeti suddenly jumped up, startling Anshuman. "I have an idea! Why don't we all meet up this weekend to decide what to do? I'm sure none of them have made solid plans for the summer, what with exams and all."

The boy's face lit up. "Yeah, that would be great! The Six back together, this time for something more exciting. I hope Nishu and Arya bring Biscuit along. He's such a cookie!"

"Ah, good old Biscuit." Preeti chuckled. "Anyways, let's finish up our work and ask Mom if we can use the tablet during break time. Then we can text everyone about the group meeting."

CHAPTER 2

THE SIX MEET UP

Mrs. Ahuja was surprised to find the kids so well-behaved and completing their chores on schedule. "On which side of the bed did I wake up this morning?" she wondered. "Regardless, I'm happy these monkeys finally got some sense."

So it was no surprise that when break time arrived, the tablet was handed over without any squabble for once. The kids quickly typed out:

"Gotta meet up. Let's meet at our usual spot tomorrow at eleven."

Elena and Roshan replied within the hour. "Sure, it's been a long time." Nishan and Arya responded later that evening.

"Sorry for the late response; had a lot of homework. Yes, we have to meet up for sure. See you tomorrow!"

"I'm so excited all of a sudden! I hope everyone shows up. We have so much to discuss." Preeti said and chuckled.

The next morning, four kids and a dog made their way to the café down the street, their usual meeting spot. "I'm pretty sure Anshu and Preeti are going to be late as usual. Why do they set the time only to show up half an hour late?" Roshan frowned.

"Well, let's order something and wait until those two show up." Elena said, heading to the counter.

"El, you literally had breakfast an hour ago. How are you hungry again?" Nishan asked.

"Try being the star swimmer at your school's swimming club. Trust me, flapping those arms and legs works up a massive appetite." Elena replied, turning to the plump man behind the counter, who greeted them with a wide grin.

"Hello, kids! Back after a long time, I see. Ah, exam season always slows down business. Not a single kid in sight, all curled up with their books from dawn to dusk. Anyways, I assume you'll have your usual?"

"You know us too well, Manohar Uncle." Roshan said, smiling as he pulled out his wallet.

"Don't pay for us, Roshan! You always pay whenever we go out. Let Nishu pay this time. He received a lot of pocket money for his birthday, and as always, his hands are burning to spend it on something useless." Arya said, glancing at her brother, who clutched his wallet and shot her an angry glare.

"This is the last time I tell you any of my plans! You knew I was planning to buy a new video game with that money."

"Woof, woof!" barked Biscuit, a golden retriever with big eyes and silky golden fur, and leapt towards Nishan, pretending to nip him.

"Yeah, yeah, Biscuit, I wouldn't dare touch a single hair on your best friend. Sometimes I feel like I've been adopted. WAIT, WHAT IF I ACTUALLY AM?!?" Nishan exclaimed, looking alarmed. The others laughed.

"Don't worry, dude. I'll pay you back after I get some money on my birthday." Roshan said with a smile.

"Fine, I'll pay this once. Actually, it's for the best. The game isn't launching until the end of the year anyway. I can always save up more by then." Nishan said, settling the bill.

Soon, they were seated around a table, munching on delicious chicken and cheese sandwiches and sipping tall glasses of icy, creamy milkshakes. Biscuit went up to shopkeeper, wagging his tail and lolling his tongue, hoping for treats. The man smiled and set down a plate of dog biscuits, watching happily as the dog proceeded to devour them in huge gulps.

"Well, now that our souls are filled to the brim, let's discuss why Anshu and Prits called this 'emergency meeting'." Elena said, finishing off the last of her sandwiches.

"I'm pretty sure it's about the summer holidays. Anshuman tried to inform me sneakily, but Preeti found out and cut him off, saying they would talk only at the group meeting." Arya replied.

"Well, we'll know what they want when they get here. Meanwhile, let's discuss our own plans for the summer..." Roshan started. Just then, Anshuman and Preeti burst into the café, panting and sweating as if chased by a monster.

"WHAT IN THE WORLD HAPPENED TO YOU TWO?!" everyone asked in unison.

"Oh, nothing much." Preeti panted. "We had just stepped out when one of the neighbor's dogs suddenly went bonkers and started chasing us. We've been running around in circles for about half an hour." She said and collapsed into a chair, out of breath.

"You should've seen her face as she screamed. She was howling as if a dinosaur were chasing us, not the neighbour's dog." Anshuman laughed. Preeti made a long face; she didn't like being the butt of the joke. "At least I wasn't the one who tumbled headfirst into the rose bushes. The poor gardener was so angry seeing his prized roses crushed that he could only wave his gardening tools and yell random words that sounded like gibberish." she said, giving a cheeky smile as she watched her brother's cheeks turn deep red in response to the children's laughter. Everyone sat down as the siblings ordered their meals.

"So, did we miss anything? School shenanigans? Cranky neighbors?" Preeti asked, helping herself to a sandwich.

"I wish there were! But clearly, exams have left no space in our brains—no room for anything else to fit in." Elena said, letting out a deep sigh.

"Yeah, this term has been really tough on me. I'll be glad to put my books away for a while." Nishan said.

"Me too." Preeti agreed, cuddling Biscuit. "As much as I love exams and assignments, it'll be a relief to take a break from the schedule."

"Anyways, let's talk about why we called you here. We've decided not to go anywhere for the holidays. We talked to our parents, and it turns out they weren't planning a trip anyway. Dad has a conference with the school board, and Mom has some big sale at her boutique. So, we were hoping you guys would be available this summer to meet up more often and do something fun." she said, both siblings looking at their friends with big, hopeful eyes.

Silence fell for a moment. Nishan was the first to speak. "We're also going nowhere. Mama will be super busy due to the heavy patient load during the summer, and Papa has been having trouble with his back lately. If anything, we were planning to talk it out with all of you today."

"I'll be here all summer as well." Elena chimed in. "Gran is unwell, so Mom has to stay with her for a few weeks while I stay at my uncle's."

The siblings' eyes lit up. "Oh my God, that's amazing! We can all meet up on the first day of the holidays and discuss what to do…"

While they were talking, Roshan sat quietly, his eyes down. The others noticed and turned to him. "What's the matter, Rosh?" Preeti asked. "Is something bothering you?"

Rosh looked up. "Yeah, I kind of have a small problem." he said.

"What is it?" everyone asked.

"I'm going somewhere this summer. The plans are almost made, and I'm pretty sure I can't ditch it even if I wanted to. I'm really sorry." he said, sounding a bit upset.

"Oh, that's absolutely fine." Elena said, trying to sound happier than she felt. "We should've asked beforehand. Anyway, where are you going?"

"Japan." Roshan replied, the frown leaving his face. "Dad has a conference, and he suggested I go with him this time so I'm not cooped up at home. I'm so excited! Visiting the famous Cherry Blossom Festival has been on my list for as long as I can remember, and now I finally get to see it in all its beauty." he said, his eyes gleaming.

"Well, too bad you won't be here with us. We'll just have to make up for your absence. Japan sounds cool, though. Too bad we can't go with you." Arya said and sighed heavily.

"Wait a minute." Rosh paused for a while, and then suddenly banged the table loudly, causing everyone to jump and nearly trample poor Biscuit.

"Oops, sorry." Rosh apologized, smiling sheepishly at the annoyed faces that looked up at him. "Guys, I just had the most brilliant idea! Why don't you all come with me… to Japan?!"

Utter silence. The kids exchanged glances. Then Elena turned to Roshan and said, "That was a good joke, but you need to work on it a bit more if you want us to laugh until we're in stitches."

"I'm not joking! We can talk to our parents and ask them to let us go together." he insisted.

"But you said your dad has already made plans. How can we be included?" Anshuman asked, scratching his forehead.

"They haven't confirmed anything yet. Dad said they'd wait until the last day of my exams to discuss and finalize everything. So, we can talk to our parents and see if we can meet next Sunday to work it all out." Rosh replied.

Another round of silence followed. Then Elena jumped up. "This is an amazing idea! Imagine if it all works out—we'd all be on a plane to Japan, having the adventure of a lifetime!" she rambled, her big eyes sparkling like diamonds.

Everyone became excited, speaking at once.

"Yeah, this all sounds amazing!"

"Yess, this is too good to be true!"

"A holiday abroad with friends? That sounds unreal!"

"Okay, so let's talk to our parents tonight and convince them to meet next weekend." Rosh said.

The kids yelled, "YES!!!" causing the poor shopkeeper, who was sorting cakes, to jump and almost trip over Biscuit again.

But Biscuit didn't mind. He joined in the excitement, wagging his tail and barking joyfully. He didn't understand the commotion, but as long as his friends were happy, he was the happiest dog in the world.

CHAPTER 3

SUMMER HOLIDAYS

Sunday dawned bright and clear. All the kids, along with their parents and Biscuit, gathered at Roshan's house to discuss the upcoming holidays.

As the adults settled in the living room, the gang and Biscuit retreated to Rosh's bedroom.

"Let's play something! Otherwise, the silence will swallow our brains. I'm pretty sure I'll faint by the time these adults finish talking. I don't remember feeling this nervous for anything in my life—not even exams." Preeti said, her palms sweating with anticipation. "Where are all the games, Rosh?"

"On the shelf beside the wardrobe." Roshan replied, his voice shaky. "I swear I'll give everything I own to God if this plan works out. What do you guys think?"

"Don't worry, Rosh. Everything will be fine. I'm sure we can go together. Our parents know we're not troublemakers." Arya said, trying to sound more reassuring than she felt.

"Except for this one." Elena said, rolling her eyes at Anshuman, who was pressed against the wall, biting his nails. "Anshu, what are you doing? And please stop chewing your nails; the sound is driving me insane."

Anshu turned around and hissed, "Shush! I'm trying to listen to what our parents are saying. For heaven's sake, Rosh, could your walls *be* any thicker? All I hear are muffled whispers!" He almost knocked over a lamp in his eagerness to eavesdrop.

Rosh frowned and turned to Preeti. "Prits, if this works out, remind me to put this guy on a leash so we don't lose him in the streets of Tokyo." He looked back at Anshu. "Fine, dig up the wall if it helps you. But seriously, stop chewing your nails. It's annoying."

"It helps me relax, just like Arya relaxes by strangling Biscuit." Anshuman quipped.

"I'm not strangling him! I just love to cuddle his huge, scruffy neck." Arya said, wrapping her arms around the dog. Biscuit let out a weak woof.

"Aaru! You are strangling him! Look, his tongue is almost touching the rug! OH MY GOD, HE'S GONNA DIE!" Nishan screamed.

"Shut up, you melodramatic queen. He's perfectly fine!" Arya said, her cheeks flushed with embarrassment. "Sorry, Biscuit.

I didn't realize I was squeezing you so tightly." She loosened her grip, and Biscuit immediately jumped on her, licking her face and letting out excited yips.

"Hmm, an overexcited dog, a strangler, a drama queen, a sticky tape and three fairly normal people losing their minds. I must say, this excitement and nervousness is having a bad effect on us." Rosh remarked, raising an eyebrow.

The longest forty-five minutes of their lives passed by slowly. The muffled conversation drove Anshu mad, while his nail-biting drove everyone else mad.

Finally, after what felt like ages, Roshan's mother peeked through the door. "Time to come out, kids!"

Whispering and murmuring nervously, the kids emerged to find their parents seated in the living room, arms and legs crossed. Arya had Biscuit on a leash to prevent any playful chaos.

Silence fell as the children's eyes met their parents'. Then Rosh's father, Vikram, spoke up. "So, we've reached a conclusion."

The kids leaned forward, anticipation written on their faces.

"We will let you go…" The children nearly burst with excitement, Arya almost sitting on Biscuit in her enthusiasm.

"But…" Nishan and Arya's mother, Rani, interrupted.

The kids groaned collectively.

"Listen to the whole thing first." said Ms. Jasmine, Elena's mother. "We'll allow you to go on this trip together, but on one condition: all of you must score well in your finals. Only then will we permit the trip."

"Consider it done." Roshan declared confidently.

"I'm not worried about any of you—except Anshu." Parineeti said, giving her son a stern look, making him shrink back behind his sister.

"I'll help him!" Preeti chimed in. "Don't worry about him. I'll make sure he studies hard and performs excellently."

"Then it's settled. Get good marks in your finals, and enjoy your vacation." Ms. Jasmine concluded.

The kids erupted with "HURRAY!" as Biscuit barked excitedly in agreement.

"Now, if you want to do well, you'd better stop this pandemonium and head to your study tables!" Jatin laughed at the chaos.

Soon, everyone said their goodbyes, and the gathering dispersed.

"Oh my God! I can't believe they actually agreed!" Anshu exclaimed that evening as they settled at their desks.

"Look, I understand this is exciting, but remember, this happiness comes with a cost. Back to studying!" Preeti said.

"Anything for a summer with friends…and JAPAN!!!" Anshu grinned, diving into memorizing tables while his sister tackled math problems.

Exam day arrived, and all the kids sat for their papers, feeling well-prepared. Two weeks of exams and preparation flew by, and finally, they were done!

With their schools following similar schedules, the kids all finished around the same time for the summer. As usual, they planned to meet up in their favorite spot to discuss their plans.

The next day, Roshan, Elena, Anshuman, and Preeti waited eagerly, but when Nishan and Arya walked in, they looked glum. Biscuit was not with them.

The others swarmed the siblings with questions.

"What happened to you both?"

"Why are you upset?"

"Where's Biscuit? Is he okay?"

"No. Biscuit had an accident last night. He slipped and fell down the stairs while going for his late-night walk and injured his foot. The vet says it's a minor fracture, but he needs about three weeks of rest and care." Arya said, her eyes brimming with tears.

Nishan comforted her. "Don't worry, Aaru. We'll call him every day and ask about him. We'll even bring him presents from Japan." Hearing this, Arya managed a small smile.

The others nodded, and while Biscuit's injury was upsetting, the thought of a summer vacation in a faraway country soon lifted their spirits.

"So here's the plan. We all leave next Wednesday with Roshan's dad and spend eight days exploring and sightseeing." Nishan said.

"Well, it'll be a bit cold there this time of year, so pack a light coat and an extra jacket or hoodie along with your normal clothes." Rosh suggested.

"Oh no!" Preeti exclaimed suddenly. "I just remembered, I don't have any socks! My feet get numb in cold weather, and I need something to cover them!"

"I don't have a coat either." Elena added. "Hey, why don't we all head to the nearest mall and buy what we need?"

Excitement erupted in a volley of exclamations.

"Yes! Great idea!"

"Let's go right now!"

"Our car can take us!"

"Wait a minute," Nishan interjected. "Who's going to pay?"

"Why, it's going to be you, obviously. You have the most allowance money right now." Arya replied with a mischievous glint in her eye.

"I am never taking out my wallet in front of you!" Nishan groaned as they all piled into the car, eager to kick off their summer holidays.

CHAPTER 4

KONNICHIWA, JAPAN!

Wednesday arrived, and the children drove to the airport with their parents, unable to sit still for a moment. After a week of packing, planning, and daydreaming about the places they would visit and the fun they would have, the excitement was palpable.

As the group stood in front of the entrance, Arya took in the bustling scene around her. She marveled at the diverse array of people coming and going. Although she had flown to different states in India, this was her first time traveling abroad.

Just then, her brother jolted her back to reality. She turned to see their parents imparting a flurry of advice.

"I've packed an extra pair of clothes in case the ones you're carrying get soiled." one parent said.

"We've labelled your suitcases to avoid any confusion at the luggage carousel." another added.

"And most importantly, keep your documents and passports in your backpacks at all times…"

The list went on, and the kids grew increasingly impatient. Finally, Roshan's dad intervened, saying, "We really have to leave now; otherwise, the plane will leave without us."

The mothers hugged their children goodbye. "Remember to call every day and update us on everything or if anything goes wrong. Have lots of fun; we'll miss you all very much."

Before parting ways, Arya whispered in her mother's ear, "Please tell Biscuit that I miss him and that I'll talk to him every day." Her mother smiled and nodded.

As the parents waved goodbye, the kids rolled their suitcases through the doorway. Soon, they were checked in and ready to board their flight to Tokyo.

As they buckled their seatbelts, Preeti turned to Elena with a chirpy voice. "I can't believe we're actually going on a trip together. I can already picture all the fun we're going to have!"

"I know, right!?" Elena replied, pressing herself into her seat. "I can sense something unexpected is going to happen on

this trip—something that will make it unforgettable. Like…
an adventure!"

"I'll be content with a normal vacation, thank you very much." Preeti said, pulling an eye mask over her eyes and slouching back in her seat. "I've worked really hard this term, and now I just want to stretch my legs and relax."

With that, the plane roared to life and took to the skies.

Eight hours later, they were in Tokyo.

As they exited the airport, a tall man dressed elegantly in a black tuxedo approached them. "*Konnichiwa!* Am I speaking to Mr. Vikram Sen, CEO of Sen & Co.?"

"This is him," Vikram said, shaking the man's hand. "And I am speaking to…?"

"Aoi Takahashi, Vice President of Murakami Industries. Welcome to Tokyo! We hope you had a comfortable flight and that you enjoy your stay." he said, bowing slightly to the children.

Remembering their manners, the kids bowed back, albeit a bit nervously.

"Please follow me. We have made all the necessary arrangements to ensure your stay in Japan will be memorable." Mr. Takahashi said, leading them to a sleek black car waiting to take them to their hotel.

As they drove past the iconic Tokyo Tower, Anshuman gazed out the window at the tall skyscrapers and orchards, all painted in vibrant shades of pink from the cherry blossoms. *Eight whole days of traveling, sightseeing, and eating with the people he loved most—everything looked too good to be true.*

CHAPTER 5

OFF TO KYOTO

The first few days in Tokyo passed uneventfully. While Vikram attended business meetings, the children explored the bustling city, visiting parks and iconic landmarks, and indulging in vast amounts of sushi.

"I never thought I would enjoy raw food this much!" Nishan exclaimed on their last day in Tokyo.

"That's why we encourage you to experiment with food more often. You never know what you might like." Elena replied.

"Oh please, I have a very developed palate." Nishan retorted, offended.

"Sure you do, for *dal-chawal*!" Arya smirked, causing the others to burst into laughter as the boy's face turned bright red.

"Let him be, guys." Roshan said. "He'll sulk for the rest of the trip if we keep teasing him. We don't want that, do we?"

"And for your kind information, I eat other things too!" Nishan protested in a squeaky voice.

Just then, Vikram peeked into their room. "I see you're all enjoying yourselves, huh? But I suggest you get some shut-eye; tomorrow's ride to Kyoto will be early. So… OFF TO BED EVERYONE!!!"

"Aye-aye, Captain!" the kids shouted, diving into their beds.

The next morning, the group gathered outside the hotel after breakfast. While they waited, a large car pulled up and stopped in front of them. A man got out and approached, catching the kids' attention. He was of average height, lean, with smooth pale skin, dressed smartly, and spoke fluent English. The gang watched as he shook hands with Roshan's father.

"Kids, this is Mr. Aki Watanabe." Vikram introduced. "He's a friend of Mr. Takahashi's, lives in Kyoto, and owns a big company there. He insisted we stay with him and his family."

Mr. Watanabe smiled warmly. "*Konnichiwa*! I'm so happy you chose to visit my hometown. We hope you enjoy your stay."

Soon, they were on the road to Kyoto. The cityscape transitioned to lush hills and sprawling fields, the countryside ablaze with cherry blossoms. The children squealed in delight as delicate petals fluttered in the wind like pink butterflies.

A little further along, Preeti spotted something in the distance and screamed in excitement, causing Mr. Watanabe to swerve slightly.

"What happened?!?" Vikram asked, turning around as the car came to a screeching halt.

"Sorry! But look, there's Mt. Fuji!" Preeti exclaimed, her eyes wide.

Everyone turned to gaze in wonder at the majestic mountain, its snow-capped peak gleaming in the sun.

"It's beautiful!"

"Stunning!"

"Awesome!"

"Did you know Mt. Fuji is 3,776 meters tall, making it the tallest mountain in Japan?" Preeti chimed in.

"Please, Prits, no one cares how much of a bookworm you are." Nishan teased, making her pout.

They resumed their journey, enjoying the scenic drive. They stopped at a small roadside restaurant for lunch, where the kids tried udon noodles for the first time. They devoured their meals, much to the amusement of Vikram and Mr. Watanabe.

"Anyone watching would think you've been starved for weeks!" Vikram laughed.

"We don't care what anyone thinks. This food is amazing! JAPAN IS…AMAAAAZING!!!" Anshuman declared, sliding back in his seat, his stomach bursting with noodles.

After a hearty lunch, the children gradually dozed off in the car. Vikram turned around and smiled at the sight of the six children, fast asleep and lost in their little worlds of wonder.

They were jolted awake about an hour later when the car suddenly stopped. Nishan and Elena fell face-first into the seats in front of them.

"Aaargghh! What happened? Have we reached?" they groaned.

"Yes. Now come out and grab your bags. I'm not carrying them all by myself!" Roshan's dad called from the back.

When they got out, they gasped at the sight before them. Aki Watanabe was wealthy! His house looked like a mansion, surrounded by orchards of mandarins, apples, pears, and peaches. In a secluded corner, giant watermelons sprawled across the ground.

"Oh my goodness, this place is huge! We could spend all day picking fruit from the trees. Look, the branches are sagging with ripe fruits!" Preeti exclaimed, her eyes gleaming.

"I can almost taste the mandarins now! YUMMMYYY!!!" Anshuman said, closing his eyes and imagining a slice of juicy fruit sliding down his gullet.

As they explored, an elderly woman emerged, holding the hands of two children. Mr. Watanabe introduced them, "Mr.

Sen, kids, this is my mother, Akane Watanabe. And these are my children, Hiroshi and Fumiko. My wife Hikari is inside cooking."

The children bowed respectfully to the old woman and waved to the kids, who smiled back. The elderly woman approached Arya, taking her hands gently. She spoke something in Japanese, leaving Arya confused.

Mr. Watanabe smiled, translating, "She says you have very pretty eyes."

"Oh, that's so nice of her! Please tell her I say thank you." Arya replied, smiling as her words were conveyed. The woman nodded, looking pleased.

A grim-looking man emerged to help with the bags. "This is Kenji. He helps around the house and tends to the orchards and gardens." Mr. Watanabe explained.

Nishan couldn't help but think Kenji resembled a villain from the anime shows he loved. The man didn't say a word, silently picked up the bags and disappeared inside.

The children felt a twinge of unease, which Mr. Watanabe quickly alleviated. "Don't worry. He's just a bit rough around the edges. He started working here last year, so he's still adjusting. But he's reliable." he assured them.

Just then, Akane said something, pointing at the kids. Hiroshi laughed and translated, "She says—ENOUGH TALKING! The kids must be hungry! Come on, let's go inside."

In their excitement to explore their new surroundings, the children hadn't noticed the sun setting behind them. It was almost evening—no wonder they felt so hungry! They were shown to their respective rooms, and soon everyone gathered around a huge table laden with a feast prepared by Mrs. Watanabe, who was an excellent cook.

As they helped themselves, Preeti turned to Elena and said, "This place is so calm and peaceful. Now I can finally enjoy the holidays the way I wanted—no schedules, no tension, *and no adventure!*"

Little did Preeti know how wrong she was about this vacation. *As the gang ate, trouble was brewing, just a few minutes away.*

CHAPTER 6

HONEN-IN

The kids woke up very late the next morning. Roshan was the first to stir, roused by the cheerful chirping of birds on the window sill. He sat up and listened for a moment before glancing at his watch—ten o'clock! Way past breakfast! He jumped out of bed and rushed to get dressed, startling Nishan and Anshuman awake.

"Get up, lazybones! We're late! Brush your teeth and get ready while I wake the girls!" he shouted as he dashed to their door.

Knocking vigorously, he could hear the bustle of activity downstairs. Everyone seemed to have been awake since sunrise. Roshan felt a hint of shame. Usually, they were usually early risers, but the holidays had made them lazy. He banged on the door again.

Elena opened it, looking disheveled. Her hair was tousled, and her eyes were half-closed. She was clearly not a morning person. "What happened? Why are you waking us up so early?" she grumbled sleepily.

"EARLY??? It's nearly lunchtime! Get ready, all three of you, if you want to eat something before lunch!" Roshan replied.

Soon, they all headed downstairs, looking fresh and clean. Mrs. Watanabe and her children greeted them warmly.

"Good morning! I hope you all slept well." She said, her smile as wide and inviting as the old woman's.

"Yes, thank you very much. I apologize for disrupting your schedule. I'm sure you're not used to guests getting up this late." Roshan said with an apologetic grin.

"Oh, don't worry about it. You're on holiday! Now, sit down and make yourselves comfortable. I've prepared a nice hot breakfast for you." she said, heading back into the kitchen.

As they settled down, Arya looked around. "Where's Uncle?"

"He and *otousan* went to Tokyo this morning. Some important work, they said. They'll be back by evening." Hiroshi replied.

Arya frowned at the unfamiliar word 'otousan' and turned to Preeti. "What does that mean?"

"It means 'father' in Japanese." Preeti explained.

Soon, a hearty breakfast arrived: bowls of steaming rice with miso soup and plates of *onigiris*, triangular rice balls stuffed with salmon. The kids' mouths watered at the sight of the lavish meal, a good sign that Mrs. Watanabe's efforts would not go in vain.

After breakfast, the kids gathered in the living room, pondering what to do for the day. Hiroshi and Fumiko joined them.

"What should we do today?" Nishan asked.

"I suggest we explore the grounds or visit some nearby spots. With both Uncle and Mr. Watanabe away, we don't have many options." Preeti said. The others nodded in agreement.

Then Elena looked around. "What about that man who helped us with our bags yesterday?"

"Oh, Kenji left for the market this morning. He said he'd be back before lunch." Hiroshi replied.

"Just as well. I didn't like the look of him. Does he always look like that?" Arya shuddered at the thought of the grim man standing in front of her.

"Yes, pretty much all the time. I've never seen him smile. He just nods and speaks in one-word replies." Fumiko added.

"Well then, let's make sure no Kenjis ruin our holiday mood. Now, back to planning!" Roshan said, prompting everyone to think again.

Suddenly, Hiroshi brightened. "I have an idea! Why don't you come with us to visit Honen-in?"

"A what 'in'?" Anshuman asked, puzzled.

"HONEN-IN! It's a shrine just a few minutes away. It's not very popular, but I promise you, it's beautiful!" Fumiko said, her face lighting up.

"Then what are we waiting for? Let's go to Honen-in!" Roshan declared, jumping to his feet.

Soon, they were trudging up the path that led to the shrine. Fumiko carried a picnic box filled with dumplings that Mrs. Watanabe had packed in case they couldn't make it back for lunch. The path climbed gently, flanked by beautiful trees and bushes. Beyond the trees lay vast fields of paddy, dotted with traditional wooden houses. Preeti and Elena inhaled deeply, savoring the fresh countryside air. "It's so pure you could almost drink it." they remarked.

"This part of the province is relatively less populated. Most of the farmers here still use traditional cultivation methods. Plus, tourism hasn't fully reached here yet. Still, quite a lot of people visit the shrine before the Cherry Blossom Festival." Hiroshi explained.

Engaged in conversation, they soon realized they had arrived at their destination.

"Here we are!" Fumiko announced.

The group found themselves in a secluded area of the woods, where silence prevailed, occasionally broken by the chirping of birds. A thatched-roof gateway beckoned them. As they crossed it, they entered an old shrine that looked like something out of a movie, with prayer halls and temples nestled on either side, cobbled pathways leading up to them. Trees in various hues surrounded them; the pink of cherry blossoms mingled with the greens and yellows of other trees, creating a captivating tapestry of nature.

As they stood spellbound, Arya heard rustling behind her and turned around, letting out a startled shriek. Everyone gathered around her to see what she was pointing at.

A pair of gleaming eyes stared out from the bushes. At first, the kids thought it was a raccoon, common in these woods. But then, a little girl emerged, dressed in nothing but a torn skirt and tank top. She sat on a rock, eyeing the children as if they were extraterrestrial beings.

"Oh, that's just little Hana." Fumiko said, letting out a sigh of relief. She turned to the girl and shouted, "Off now!"

Hana jumped on the rock, glanced back one last time, and scurried away like a wildcat.

"Who was that?" Preeti asked.

"That's Hana." Fumiko explained. "She lives in a nearby hut with her grandmother. They come over sometimes to help pick fruit. She's a real wild one, always skipping school to roam the woods."

"Actually, it's her grandmother we're going to visit now. It's our last stop before heading back for lunch. She tells great stories about the shrine. You'll love hearing them." Hiroshi said as they made their way down the path.

"Will we be able to understand her?" Preeti inquired.

"You'll be fine. She went to school when she was little, so she can speak a bit of broken English. You'll understand her just fine." Hiroshi reassured them.

"Great! Let's go hear Grandma's tale!" Roshan said, skipping happily ahead.

Oh, she'll tell a tale alright. *A tale, you'll never forget.*

CHAPTER 7

THE TALE OF HARUTO

The kids continued walking down the path until they came to a small clearing just a few feet off the road. In the middle stood a small hut made of wooden planks, surrounded by trees on all sides. An old woman sat in front, knitting. She looked up and smiled when she saw the group of children approaching.

She said something in Japanese to Fumiko, who replied in kind. To the Six, it all sounded foreign. They looked at Preeti.

"What? Why do you expect me to understand their conversation? I haven't learned anything except 'hello,' 'goodbye,' and 'nice to meet you'." she snapped, feeling annoyed and embarrassed for not being able to understand.

As they squabbled, Fumiko called out, "She's asking us to come and sit down!"

They gathered in a half-circle around her. Then, Hana's face suddenly appeared on a rock nearby. At first, she seemed apprehensive of the crowd. She cautiously walked over and looked at each of them, as if to say, "I know both of you, but who are these new ones?" Still maintaining her distance, she settled down near her grandmother's knee.

The old lady spoke. "Welcome. I am happy you came. Would you like something to eat?" she asked in a sweet voice.

"No, thank you for asking. We had a pretty late breakfast. We have some dumplings with us, though. We'd be more than glad to share." Roshan said, flashing a broad smile. He liked this lady, with her wrinkled face and soothing demeanor.

"Thank you. You are a very good boy." she said, smiling back. The others looked at Roshan with admiration; he always had a way of speaking with grown-ups that made them value his words.

"*Obaasan*, tell them the story you always tell us when we visit, the one about the shrine." Fumiko said.

"Yes, yes, I will tell them the story. It is very interesting. Listen carefully." The kids leaned in, eager to hear as the lady began her narration.

"Long ago, there lived a great samurai named Haruto Yamamoto. He was very brave and very dangerous. He excelled in battle and soon became popular throughout

Japan. The Emperor asked to see him and made him his favorite. Haruto grew rich and amassed great wealth. But then he became afraid—afraid of people trying to steal his treasure. So he decided to hide it somewhere safe, somewhere no one would ever think to look."

"Where?" Nishan asked, almost tumbling forward in his impatience.

"He hid it in the shrine! In a *kinko-shitsu*, under one of the temples. Yes, he hid it!" the woman exclaimed, her eyes wide.

The Six looked at Hiroshi, puzzled by the term "kinko-shitsu." He clarified, "It means a vault. She's saying Haruto buried the treasure in an underground vault beneath the shrine."

"Yes." the old lady confirmed. "He buried it. And then he cursed it!"

"What curse?" Anshuman asked.

"A curse that every full moon, the earth would shake, and the spirit of the temple would rise and float as a warning to those who seek the treasure. Those who still look will DIE!" The old lady's tone was serious, her hands trembling.

"Damn, that man was a snob! Imagine cursing a whole shrine for a treasure. Thank goodness it's just a story." Elena said, finding the tale rather phony.

"This isn't just a story, not just a story at all." the woman replied, pulling the girl closer. She glanced around as if watching for eavesdroppers, then spoke in a low voice. "Last full moon, I SAW IT! I felt the earth shake, and then I saw a white light—the TEMPLE, FLOATING!"

CHAPTER 8

BACK HOME

The children suddenly shivered in the April sunshine. What did the woman mean? Did the shrine really rise up and float on a full moon night?

"Are you sure you saw the shrine rise into the air? Perhaps you were just dreaming." Arya said, almost shaking with fear.

"No, no! I saw the temple floating! Last full moon, I sat outside looking at the stars. Suddenly, I felt the ground shake. I thought maybe it was an earthquake. But then I saw a bright glow in the sky, and I saw the clear image of the temple slowly rising. Someone was looking for the treasure. Someone who could destroy us all!" the old lady screamed, sounding like a witch trying to cast a spell on the kids.

Roshan decided it was time to go.

"Thank you for the wonderful story, but we really need to head back if we want to make it in time for lunch." he said, noticing Arya and Preeti growing scared. He held Arya's hand and signaled for the others to get up. They stood, bowed respectfully to the woman, and began walking home.

"Thank you for coming! Come back anytime! And BEWARE!" the woman called after them.

"Well, that was an interesting story. That woman is one heck of a storyteller." said Elena, seemingly unfazed.

"What did she mean by seeing the temple float in the air? You don't think it's real, do you, Rosh?" Arya asked, almost digging her nails into Nishan's arm, making him wince.

"Absolutely not! This story was probably created by the village folk years ago to stop children from wandering out at night. If it were real, Hiroshi and Fumiko would have seen it too." Roshan replied.

"Well, we weren't here last full moon." Fumiko said. "We were visiting our uncle in Kyushu for the month. But for all I know, this whole thing is probably not true. The peculiar thing is she's never mentioned this before."

"Well, she did say she saw it last full moon, about a month ago. But I think the poor lady has narrated the story so many times that she has begun to envision it as true." Elena said.

That evening, when the adults returned, the kids recounted the day's events.

"A shrine in the air!? Well, that's a first. Sounds like an interesting tale." Vikram laughed.

"She makes the tale sound so real! She used to tell it to me and my sister every night at bedtime. We'd fall asleep dreaming of spirits and gold coins." Mr. Watanabe reminisced.

"Yes, but I'm pretty sure she never mentioned a floating shrine, did she?" Roshan asked.

"Enough of this shrine talk; it's giving me a headache." Vikram said. "Anyway, we have something important to tell you. Both of us have to go to Tokyo for a few days. Some important work came up, and I won't be able to stay for the rest of this trip." He looked apologetic.

The children groaned.

"But don't worry. I'll try and join you on the last day of the trip. In the meantime, you can continue your stay here and explore nearby spots. I see you're enjoying your time here, aren't you?" Vikram said.

"But Dad…," Roshan began, but Mrs. Watanabe, having overheard the conversation, interrupted.

"Let them go, dear. We can have our own fun. Hiroshi and Fumiko can take you sightseeing, and there's fruit-picking day after tomorrow. I'm sure you'll have a great time helping in the gardens." she said with a smile.

"Well, I guess work is more important after all." Roshan said, wrapping his arms around his father. "Please come back as soon as possible. I'll miss you so much." Vikram smiled.

"Thank you, son. I'll leave tonight. Don't worry; I'll try to return as soon as I can." He then handed Roshan a phone. "Keep this. You can use it to contact your families and take pictures. My number is your emergency contact; just call me if you need anything."

Mrs. Watanabe turned to her children. "I won't be here tonight. I'm taking your grandmother over to your aunt's place in town and will be staying overnight. I'll be back tomorrow morning. Dinner is already served. Can you hold the fort while I'm gone?" she asked.

"Sure we can." Hiroshi replied. "Don't worry; we'll take care of the house."

"Make sure to lock the front door and leave the back door slightly open. Kenji is out for a stroll and will be back late."

After a while, the adults headed out, and the children shut the gates and locked all the doors and windows. As instructed, Hiroshi left the back door slightly ajar for Kenji to return after his late-night stroll.

After dinner, everyone gathered in the hall to play games. When the clock struck ten, Roshan stood up. "Day's over, people. Into your pajamas and into bed!" he commanded, sounding like a captain.

"Aye-aye, Captain!" the others replied, marching off to their rooms.

Soon, they were getting ready for bed. Just before turning in, Arya approached Roshan and asked for the phone. "Just for a few minutes. I haven't talked to Biscuit in a couple of days." she said, looking at him with pleading eyes.

The boy smiled and handed her the phone. "How's he doing? Is his foot healing?"

"He still walks with a limp, but the last visit to the vet showed that his foot is almost healed. Another week or two of proper rest, and he should be just fine." she chirped happily.

After a while, all the lights went out, and soon everyone was in bed, snoring away. No one heard the back door shut. No one heard footsteps walking down the path behind the house. No one even heard the faint rumble as the ground shook lightly.

CHAPTER 9

IN THE MIDDLE OF
THE NIGHT

After a few hours had passed, Nishan suddenly woke up. He felt something unusual and glanced at the clock, still half-asleep. Two in the morning. "Must've been a dream." he thought, and lay back in bed.

But just as he was about to drift off again, it happened! A rumbling sound shook the ground. The boy sprang up in terror. Seeing the whole room tremble, he started screaming.

"EARTHQUAKE!!! WE HAVE TO GET OUT!"

Roshan and Anshuman nearly fell off their beds, startled by Nishan's sudden cries. The shaking stopped just as they woke up.

"What happened, Nishu?" Anshuman asked, rubbing his sleepy eyes. "Why are you shouting in the middle of the night? Did you have a nightmare?"

"Earthquake! We must run outside!" Nishan almost shouted into Roshan's ear.

"Now you listen, you...." Roshan began indignantly, but then it started again! The rumble returned, and the ground shook violently, as if a giant drill was boring into the earth beneath them.

"Rosh, I'm scared. What's happening?" Anshuman said, clutching the boy's arm.

"Don't panic! Just get out of the building as soon as possible. I'll get the girls." Roshan said, sprinting out.

As they raced outside, he yelled at the top of his lungs, "Preeti, Elena, Arya! Get out of the house… NOW!"

Preeti woke up, grabbed Arya's hand, and ran out of the room, followed closely by Elena. They bumped into the Watanabe kids in the hallway.

"What in the name of chocolate fudge is happening?!" Anshuman asked, frightened.

"Probably an earthquake. Better get out before the house comes down and makes toast out of us!" Fumiko said, and they dashed for their lives.

The tremors stopped as soon as they stepped into the open air.

Everyone stood still for a moment, too stunned to speak. Then Arya looked up and called out, "Uh guys, look up at the moon. You might want to see this."

Everyone looked up, and their eyes widened in shock. Shining above them, illuminating the night sky, was a full moon!

They exchanged glances. Did it mean…? No, it couldn't be true. Surely this was just a coincidence.

They didn't have to wait long to confirm their suspicions, for, moments later, a bright light suddenly lit up the sky, blinding them. It seemed to be coming from the direction of the shrine.

Once their eyes adjusted to the brightness, they were dumbfounded. Nishan's mouth dropped open like a goldfish.

The shrine was floating in the air!

The mystical sight lingered over the woods for a few minutes, and then, as the group watched, it began to fade from the night sky.

As darkness enveloped the sky once again, the kids stared at one another in disbelief.

"Was all of that real? I highly doubt any of it was." Preeti said, her voice trembling.

"I'm pretty sure I'm still dreaming. Someone pinch me, please." Nishan said. Elena decided to fulfill his request and pinched his cheek hard. He let out a yelp.

"YEEOOWW!!! THAT HURT!" he exclaimed, rubbing the spot, which had turned a bright red.

"All of this is very strange. First the story, then the shaking, and now the floating shrine. From what I understand, this is all a mystery—*a real mystery*!"

CHAPTER 10

A REAL MYSTERY

The Six, along with Hiroshi and Fumiko, stood perplexed. None of the events from just moments ago made any sense. Everything felt too unnatural to believe.

"I must say, this feels very strange. Something is going on—something beyond our understanding. But for now, I suggest we get some sleep. We have to rise early for fruit picking. We can discuss everything over lunch." Fumiko proposed.

As they headed back inside, Hiroshi added, "Let me check on Kenji real quick. It's intriguing that he slept through the entire thing."

He approached Kenji's door and was puzzled to find it slightly open. Peeking into the dark room, he saw Kenji sprawled on the bed, covered in a huge blanket. The man snored so loudly it sounded like a cow in distress.

"Damn, that man can sleep!" Hiroshi thought, chuckling to himself as he closed the door quietly behind him.

The next morning, sun rays streamed through the windows, illuminating the room. Arya woke up and glanced at her watch: seven in the morning. They had barely slept for five hours.

As she lay in bed, replaying the previous night's events, a knock on the door interrupted her thoughts.

"Hey, Aaru, Prits, El! Time to get ready! IT'S FRUIT PICKING DAY!" Roshan called out.

Soon, the children, Mrs. Watanabe, and Kenji were out in the gardens. Hana and her grandmother joined them, looking cheerful. Mrs. Watanabe had called them over to help pick fruit, relishing the lively atmosphere that had been missing for so long.

As they settled into their tasks, the old woman shot a knowing glance at the Six. They exchanged looks, silently acknowledging that she too, had witnessed the floating shrine.

The group spent the morning in the gardens. Roshan, Hiroshi, and Elena knocked fruits down with pointed sticks, while Fumiko, Arya, and the old lady gathered them into baskets and crates. Preeti labeled each crate, and at the far end of the garden, Nishan, Anshuman, and Kenji picked watermelons. Hana climbed trees like a monkey, reaching for the fruits that were out of reach.

By noon, they had accomplished a lot. The gang helped separate the baskets: some for storage in the pantry, others for the farmers' market.

After finishing, they sat down under a tree, exhausted but satisfied. Mrs. Watanabe emerged with tall glasses of lemonade. "I'm so grateful to all of you. You've really helped us out. Here's some lemonade to refresh you." she said with a warm smile.

"Where's Kenji?" Hiroshi asked.

"Oh, he took all the fruits to the market. He won't be back until sunset." she replied before heading back inside.

The old lady joined them under the tree, and soon Hana joined in too. They began discussing the previous night's events.

"So you believe me now?" the lady said, pride shining in her eyes.

"Hmm… seems part of the story is real after all." Roshan mused. "I thought about it all night and came up with two explanations. First, perhaps we've all lost our minds. Second, someone might actually be trying to seek Haruto Yamamoto's legendary treasure. One thing's for sure: the spirit isn't real!"

Everyone fell silent for a moment. Then Preeti asked, "What do you mean the spirit isn't real? We saw it with our own eyes!"

"We certainly did. But I think the 'spirit' might've been a hologram, projected on a large scale to scare people away from the shrine." Roshan said confidently.

"How can you be so sure?" Elena asked skeptically.

"I've studied projections and holograms. If I'm right, while the treasure story might hold some truth, the spirit is most likely a hoax."

"And what about the shaking? How do you explain the tremors we felt?" Nishan pressed.

"Most likely, some sort of mechanism. They might have drilled deep into the earth to produce shockwaves."

"Well, if any of this is true, it has to stop immediately." Fumiko said, concerned. "I heard people gossiping about the shrine on my way to the market this morning. The sudden appearance of the 'spirit' has baffled them. Many families are considering moving to the city to avoid any trouble, which would severely impact the local economy."

"The villagers can be dealt with later." Roshan said, determination in his voice. He stood up, energized. "The first thing we need to do is investigate the shrine!"

CHAPTER 11

BACK AT THE SHRINE

The seven children stared at Roshan, confused. What did he mean by investigating the mystery of the shrine?

"Surely you don't mean *us* going over there to investigate, do you?" Nishan asked; with a half a mind to run all the way back to India if Roshan even suggested such a thing.

"Yes," came Roshan's firm reply.

"Hold up, mister! No way in hell am I okay with this!" Nishan snapped. "We're not detectives. We're just kids! Kids are supposed to sleep and eat on vacation, not snoop around floating places!"

"I agree with Nishu." Preeti added. "Rosh, think this through. We're not built for this investigation stuff. Let the real detectives handle it. Why drag ourselves into something potentially risky and life-threatening?"

"Come on, guys. We should help however we can. The people here have been kind to us since day one. Now it's our turn to restore peace in their minds by unravelling these mystical happenings." Roshan insisted.

"I agree with Roshan. Count me in." Elena said, her eyes sparkling with excitement. "If this turns out to be a hoax, I want to give those tricksters a piece of my mind for ruining my sleep!"

"I'll help too! This sounds thrilling!" Anshuman squeaked, practically bouncing with enthusiasm.

Arya remained silent for a moment, then said, "This sounds scary, but if Rosh is there to protect me, I'm scared of nothing!" She smiled. "Count me in too!"

The four of them turned to Nishan and Preeti.

"Ughh!" Nishan groaned. "Well, I guess I have no choice but to join, now that Aaru's in. I don't want to be the odd one out."

Preeti sighed. "I still think it's a bad idea, but I'd hate to miss out on anything. So, I'm coming too!"

"We'll help as well." Hiroshi added, with Fumiko nodding. "This is our home, and we won't let anyone drive us out."

"Good. I guess we're having an adventure after all! Wow, it feels cool just saying that. Now, back to business. We'll arrange a picnic in the woods near the shrine."

Mrs. Watanabe raised an eyebrow at the sudden picnic idea. "Are you sure you don't want to eat in? It's a bit chilly today. I was planning to cook some steaming hot ramen and *yakitori* for all of you." she said, slightly disappointed.

"It's all right, *okaasan*." Fumiko said quickly. "We haven't had a proper outing since Roshan and his friends arrived. Since they'll be leaving soon, we thought a stroll in the woods and a picnic would be perfect. We'll be back by sunset." She crossed her fingers, wishing upon her forefathers that her mother would agree.

Thankfully, Mrs. Watanabe agreed, and soon they were headed back to the shrine, a massive picnic basket dangling over Hiroshi's shoulder. Mrs. Watanabe had packed tuna rolls and several slices of *okonomiyaki*—a savory pancake stuffed with vegetables.

When they reached the entrance, Roshan turned around. "We should find a clearing to set up our picnic. If anyone suspicious comes by, the picnic will make us look like harmless kids just enjoying a hike."

Everyone began searching for the perfect spot. Soon, Anshuman's voice called out from behind some bushes, "Guys, I found the perfect spot! It's right by these bushes!"

The others peeked over to find a small clearing, a few feet from the entrance. Surrounded by bushes, it felt cozy.

"It seems perfect. It's not too hidden, but just enough for us to keep an eye out for anything suspicious. Plus, the bushes will shelter us from the cold winds." Preeti said as they began to set up.

As they unpacked the carpets and dishes, a sudden rustling noise startled them. Something sprang down from a nearby tree and landed on Nishan's back.

He screamed and started running around, "HELP!!! I've been attacked by a monkey! It's gonna bite my neck!"

The others looked up and, to his surprise, burst into laughter. The "monkey" on his back also started giggling. It was Hana!

"Get off me, you giant lemur!" Nishan said, shaking her off. Hana pointed excitedly at one of the temples, as if something was hidden there.

The children understood her enthusiasm but decided to wait for the right moment. "We'll search every nook and corner…" Hiroshi said, pulling out the tuna rolls. "…but not before LUNCH! Come on, let's eat!"

Everyone, including Hana, sat down to enjoy the scrumptious spread. The tuna rolls tasted heavenly. Nishan quickly devoured more than half the food and sighed in satisfaction. "This is what paradise must taste like. Why can't we have meals like this more often?"

"Maybe because we don't live here, and our parents wouldn't often let us eat meals like these." Arya replied with a chuckle.

"Cheeky, aren't you?" he shot back, making a face.

After finishing their meal, they cleaned up and ventured inside the shrine. Once inside, Roshan said, "Split up and search every corner. Keep your eyes and ears open. I bet something here will catch our attention. And Aaru, watch out for any strangers that might be roaming around."

They spread out, searching every nook and corner. They looked behind bushes, tapped walls, checked under rocks, and even lifted some stone statues, hoping to find a clue.

After about an hour, exhaustion began to set in. They had searched everywhere and found nothing.

"Maybe this was all a prank to scare the villagers." Anshuman suggested, panting.

"Yeah, I think you're right. Let's go." Roshan said, disheartened. They began to head out.

Just then, Hana came up and tugged at Preeti's dress. "What happened?" she asked. Then her eyes fell on the little girl's fist. It was clenched shut.

Curious, she gently pried it open. Everyone gasped as they saw a gold coin nestled in Hana's palm!

They stood in stunned silence, then Fumiko took the coin and examined it closely. "It's real! So the story of the treasure might be true after all."

All eyes turned to Hana. "Where did you find the coin? Take us there!" Hiroshi urged, barely containing his excitement.

Hana led the way, and soon they found themselves at what appeared to be a dead end behind the main prayer hall. Elena peeked around the structure and gestured for the others to come over.

Behind the walls, concealed by creepers and ivy, stood a rock-like structure, protruding from the ground. An outline ran along the inner edges, resembling the sealed mouth of a cave.

"Look!" Preeti pointed at the entrance. "The area around this rock is less overgrown than the rest of the shrine. Almost as if someone cleared it to reveal the entrance and then covered it with ivy after their little odyssey to fool tourists into thinking it's just a rock."

"From what I gather, these people aren't mere tricksters; they're treasure hunters! And they won't stop until they have the treasure for themselves!" A chill ran down Roshan's spine as he spoke.

As they processed these clues, a shrill shout suddenly pierced the air, shattering the silence. They turned to see a man walking briskly toward them, waving his fists angrily. *"Hey, all of you! Clear off this instant!"*

CHAPTER 12

THE SIX ARE SUSPICIOUS

The man appeared to be American, tall, and sporting a piercing voice with an unmistakable accent. He wore a cotton T-shirt, cargo shorts, and a cap, giving him a casual yet authoritative look.

He stormed up to the kids, fuming. "What do you think you're doing, trespassing on this property? Children aren't allowed in here!"

Roshan noticed Anshuman and Arya looking frightened and stepped forward to confront the man. "Are you sure? Because we've been visiting this place for quite a while now, and no one has warned us this is private property."

"Oh, this place is the government's, all right. It's been sealed off for excavations." the man replied, clearly annoyed by Roshan's defiance.

"That's odd." Hiroshi chimed in. "If there were any excavations or archaeological work happening, the authorities would have sent out announcements to warn locals to steer clear of the site."

"Well, I'm telling you to steer clear!" the man nearly howled, his voice rising.

"And who are you exactly to order us around?" Roshan challenged, narrowing his eyes. Something about this man felt off.

"I'm an archaeologist. I've been sent here to assess the excavation. And I need all of you to get out of here!" he said, his irritation evident.

"Lower your voice, sir!" Roshan replied firmly but respectfully. "We're just harmless kids exploring. Our friends brought us here to show us this beautiful place. If there was an excavation, we would've been notified days ago. And as far as excavation is concerned....I don't see any signs of work—no mud, no digging, nothing."

The man seemed taken aback. "Wh-what do you mean? You don't believe me?!"

"Not until you show us proper identification proving you're a real archaeologist and not just one of those lunatics digging up ruins under the guise of research." Elena added, her voice steady.

The man's face turned purple with rage, his expression resembling an angry bull. He struggled for words, clearly flustered. Hiroshi, sensing the tension, nudged Roshan.

Understanding the signal, Roshan said curtly, "Fine, we'll get going. Not because we're scared, but because you've bored us to the point of losing interest in further exploration. Come on, guys; let's head back to our picnic. Let the madman find his words." He let out a final huff and turned to leave.

As the man stood there, bewildered, the kids marched out one by one. Roshan gestured for them not to look back. They stepped out with heads held high, though Arya, Anshuman, and Preeti felt shaken. Who was this man, and what was he doing here? He certainly didn't look like a archaeologist.

Once they reached their picnic spot, Roshan turned around and asked. "Quick, where's the coin? Where is it?!"

Fumiko handed him the coin, and he sighed in relief. "Thank God you still had it! Are you sure he didn't see it?"

"No, I tucked it into my pocket the moment I heard him." Fumiko reassured him. "That man can't even conceal his true identity!"

Arya looked astonished. "What do you mean? Was he a police officer?"

Elena chuckled. "No, Aaru. He was neither an archaeologist nor a police officer. He was a trickster!"

"A TRICKSTER!?" Arya exclaimed, her eyes wide.

"Yeah, a trickster." Preeti explained. "People who fool others to cause trouble."

"How do you know he was a trickster?" Anshuman asked, curious.

Preeti laid out her observations. "He looked too…white to be an archaeologist. Most archaeologists are tanned from working in the sun for hours. His hands and legs had no bruises or scars from digging."

"He's probably involved in this whole shrine mystery!" Anshuman concluded.

"Probably." Roshan said, deep in thought. "If he thinks he's gotten rid of us, too bad for him! We'll beat him at his own game! I've got an idea!" His eyes sparkled with mischief.

The others looked at him, intrigued. *What scheme did the boy have up his sleeve this time?*

CHAPTER 13

SNEAKING OUT

The others stared at Roshan, eager to hear his plan. "We should sneak out tonight and explore that opening. It probably leads to the vault containing the treasure." He said.

Silence enveloped the group. Finally, Fumiko spoke up, uncertainty in her voice. "Are you sure we should sneak out at night? It sounds risky."

Roshan explained, his tone serious. "We need to take risks if we want a permanent solution to this problem. Who knows if those men will stop at just scaring people away? They might even blow up the shrine to get to the treasure. We can't let that happen, can we?"

Preeti shuddered at the thought. The idea of the shrine being razed to the ground was too disturbing to contemplate.

"Here's the plan." Roshan continued. "I suggest we sneak out after midnight when all the lights are off, and your mom and Kenji will be asleep. That way, we can go unnoticed."

Nishan's eyes sparkled with excitement. "Yeah, that sounds good! We'll have dinner, play some games, and then pretend to go to bed. Once it's dark, we can start our nighttime adventure!"

"Exactly. It's better if we sneak out through the back door; it's a quicker path to the shrine." Fumiko added.

Roshan nodded, then suggested, "I think it would be better if we didn't all go searching for the treasure at once."

The others exchanged glances. "What do you mean?" Elena asked.

"Nine kids is too large a group for a treasure hunt at night. We'd be too easy to spot. It's best if we split into smaller groups."

Everyone agreed. "So which group does what?" Preeti asked.

"Let's discuss the details somewhere private, like at home." Roshan suggested, glancing at the man emerging from the shrine, casting a wary eye in their direction. "Let's pack up and head back. Remember to ignore him."

As they walked by, they could feel the man's angry gaze on them. Anshuman nearly tripped, trying not to giggle.

Back at home, they quickly took care of their chores—helping in the kitchen, watering plants, tidying up the living room etc.

As the sun began to set, they made their final preparations. Hiroshi gathered torches while Fumiko packed cakes and chocolates from the pantry, just in case they got hungry during their adventure.

When darkness fell, Roshan called for a final meeting in the girls' room. "What's the update? Everything ready?" he asked as they convened.

Hiroshi reported, "Yes, everything's ready. The torches are packed, and we have several bottles of water, food and a first aid kit in case anyone gets hurt."

"Perfect. Here's the plan: we'll split into three groups. Hiroshi, Nishan, Elena, and I will explore the opening at the back of the shrine. Anshu and Preeti will stay outside to look for clues. Fumiko and Arya will keep an eye on the house in case someone wakes up."

"But why can't I come with you?" Arya asked, looking disappointed.

"We need someone to fetch help if we run into trouble, and you're the most sensible of us all." Roshan replied, placing a reassuring hand on her shoulder. She managed a small smile.

After dinner, they played games with the Watanabe kids until a quarter to ten. Once they helped clean up, they wished everyone goodnight and went upstairs to their rooms.

Hours later, as the clock ticked close to midnight, Roshan quietly got up and slipped into the corridor. He softly knocked on the girls' door. "It's almost midnight. Are you all set?"

"Almost done! Be out in a minute." Preeti called from inside.

Soon, the six of them were tiptoeing down the stairs, careful to avoid creaky steps. They had all worn their jackets over their clothes to stay warm. Waiting for them downstairs were Hiroshi and Fumiko.

"Coast is clear." Hiroshi whispered, handing them torches. "Mom and Kenji are fast asleep. We're good to go."

"Wait!" Arya paused, a thought crossing her mind. "How will we keep in touch?"

"I've got this." Roshan said, pulling out his mobile phone. "You didn't think I'd leave without it, did you?"

"And there's a phone in our room. You can use that to call if anything happens." Fumiko added.

"Okay, let's go have an adventure!" Roshan exclaimed, leading them to the back door. To their surprise, it was already open.

"Who opened it?" Anshuman asked, wide-eyed. "Was it you, Hiroshi?"

"No, I didn't. Maybe Kenji forgot to latch it when he locked up." Hiroshi said. "Either way, we can't waste time."

As they stepped outside, Arya called after them, "Please come back safe!"

Nishan turned around, hugging his sister tightly. "Don't worry, Aaru. We'll be fine. Remember, we still have to get presents for Biscuit!"

Arya nodded, and the two girls watched as the silhouettes of the six children faded into the night, six pinpoints of light gliding down an invisible path towards their adventure.

CHAPTER 14

FUMIKO FINDS OUT

The six children trudged through the dark lane, flanked by overgrown bushes. The moonlight cast eerie shadows, and the occasional flicker of a lamp post barely illuminated their path.

"What were we thinking, hiking in the dark for a few trinkets? I should've known better. Oh God, save us from eternal doom!" Nishan exclaimed, throwing his hands up dramatically.

"Stop being a *nautanki*, Nishu." Roshan huffed, exhausted from the day's earlier adventures. "It's just a teeny-tiny nighttime exploration. Trust me, nothing bad is going to happen."

Preeti raised an eyebrow at him. "Who warned you that this idea sucks? If only you'd listened to my advice. Now it's no use crying over spilled milk. Let's just get through this night. I need to sleep by six in the morning!"

Back at the house, Arya kept glancing at the big clock in the living room. She and Fumiko sat with their torches switched on, careful not to turn on any lights lest it woke up Mrs. Watanabe.

"It's been twenty minutes since they left. Haven't they reached yet?" Arya asked, trying to distract herself by making shadow bunnies with the torchlight.

"The road is short but overgrown." Fumiko replied. "They'll need to be super careful not to disturb any animals that might be resting."

"I'm so bored! What should we do? We can't just sit here all night!" Arya said, and let out a big yawn.

Fumiko considered it. "You can sleep in my room. We don't both need to stay awake all night. We can take turns keeping watch."

"Sounds good. Better than doing nothing!" Arya agreed.

"Great, you go to sleep. I'll wake you up at two for the next watch."

As Arya settled in, Fumiko picked up a book, reading by the torchlight. An hour passed, and suddenly, her torch flickered ominously. "Great! Hiroshi always forgets to replace the batteries. I hope the others don't suffer like me. Now what do I do?"

Suddenly, a light bulb went off in her head. "Kenji might have some batteries in his bedside drawer. I saw him take some out a couple of weeks ago. I hope he won't mind me borrowing a few."

Tiptoeing to his room, she found the door unlocked. As she turned the knob, it creaked softly. Inside, Kenji lay asleep, snoring loudly under his covers.

"I need to ask him how to sleep like that." Fumiko whispered to herself and giggled, imagining the grumpy man sharing tips on snoring.

While she rummaged through the drawer for batteries, something clattered to the floor with a metallic thud. Panic surged as she feared it might wake Kenji. She quickly knelt down to find it, praying he hadn't heard.

Then she spotted something glinting near the bed. Leaning closer, she illuminated it with her dimming torch. A gasp of horror escaped her lips—it was a gold coin, identical to the one they had found at the shrine that afternoon!

Confusion flooded her mind. How could Kenji have the exact same coin? Even stranger, what was a gold coin from Honen-in doing in the housekeeper's bedside drawer?

Forgetting all about the batteries, she shone her torch around the room, hoping to find some clues. Suddenly something on the study table caught her eye. Coming closer, she saw a few charts sprawled out. They looked like the blueprints of a building complex.

She read the labels on the diagrams carefully: "Entrance, Pathway, Hall, Opening…" Opening!? Why did that ring a bell? Of course, the opening of a cave! Was it possible that this was… No, surely it couldn't be.

At that moment, Fumiko was practically trembling. She crept closer to the sleeping figure, hesitating for a moment before suddenly throwing off the sheets. Instead of Kenji, she found a couple of bolsters arranged to look like a sleeping man, and a speaker nearby was blasting out snoring sounds.

In an instant, everything clicked into place. She had figured out the entire mystery.

Without wasting another second, Fumiko raced across the hall to her room. Bursting through the door, she shook Arya awake.

"What happened?" Arya mumbled, startled to find Fumiko looking pale and frantic.

"Quick, call Rosh! Our friends might be in danger!" Fumiko urged, her heart pounding.

CHAPTER 15

INSIDE THE OPENING

The six children trekked along the overgrown path, clearing away creepers and branches that obstructed their way.

"Are we there yet? I'm pretty sure my trousers are ripped on one side!" Anshuman complained.

"Almost there. Hang in there, buddy." Roshan reassured him, glancing ahead.

Finally, they emerged onto the main road leading to the shrine, just past the clearing where the old lady lived. Rosh scanned the area; the lights were out. The woman and her little girl were likely fast asleep. He felt a mix of relief and guilt for having convinced Hana to stay behind.

"Not that she's weak, but we don't necessarily need her help. We're plenty as it is." he thought.

As they passed through the gate, Elena scanned the courtyard. An eerie silence surrounded the shrine, as if none of the earlier chaos had ever happened.

Suddenly, something rustled in the bushes behind Preeti. She jumped back in fright, bumping into Anshuman.

"What are you doing?" he snapped, exasperated. "I was about to fall over. Do you plan on breaking my nose?"

"Sorry! But I heard rustling in the bushes back there. Maybe someone's hiding!" Preeti glanced nervously around.

"It's a bush, Prits, not a palace. It can't hide a whole person! Probably just a rabbit." he replied, rolling his eyes. "Let's join the others."

They regrouped, all staring at the entrance, contemplating how to open it.

"Well, now that we've reached, it's time to part ways, Prits and Anshu. Remember to search every corner of the shrine. If you find any object that seems suspicious, pick it up and place it carefully in your handkerchief." Roshan instructed. "And here, take this." He said, handing his phone to Preeti, "Use it to call for help if needed."

"We'll try our best. Take it easy, guys. Be safe in there!" Anshuman said with a smile before joining his sister.

Turning back to the entrance, Roshan examined it closely. He slid his fingers between the stones, searching for a latch or bolt, but found nothing.

"There must be a lever or switch to open this." Elena suggested, scrutinizing the structure. "It looks mechanically operated."

"Good idea! Let's look for it. There has to be one hidden nearby." Roshan agreed.

As they searched, Hiroshi suddenly spotted a niche in the wall, almost completely hidden by ivy. He approached it, brushing aside the leaves. Inside, he saw an iron rod jutting from the damp ground, ornately carved with various motifs. Despite the moisture around it, the iron looked clean, with only the bottom showing signs of rust.

"Almost as if someone restored it for use." he thought, excitement bubbling within him. "Guys, I think I found the lever!"

Roshan hurried over, joined by Elena and Nishan. When they saw the iron rod, their eyes widened in amazement.

"Yeah, it looks like a lever." Roshan said, inspecting it. "It must have been used by the warrior to open the vault." He gripped the lever. "Time to step into Haruto Yamamoto's shoes. Let's fire this thing up!"

He pulled with all his strength, but it didn't budge. He tried again, more determined this time. Still no luck.

"Heavy shoes, are they?" Nishan quipped, prompting a chuckle from the group. Roshan shot him a scornful look.

"Sarcastic, aren't you? Now help me. This thing must take an army to pull."

They all wrapped their hands around the lever and pulled with all their might. The iron remained stubbornly still.

"Okay, one more time. Come on, guys! WE CAN DO IT! PULL!!!"

The group gave it everything they had, and suddenly, the lever gave way and tilted forward. They stumbled back from the force, gasping as they regained their balance.

Nothing happened for a moment. Then, a grating sound echoed as the rock began to shake. Nishan dug his nails into Hiroshi's arm.

"What's happening?" he asked, his voice trembling.

Elena went up to the rock and peered closely. She let out a low whistle.

"Guys, the opening has bulged out! There's a gap right behind it." She shone her torch into the darkness. "Looks like a tunnel. What it leads to, I have no clue."

"There's only one way to find out." Roshan said, his torch held high.

As they stepped into the tunnel, they were amazed to see natural caves carved out by running water over the years.

"So I guess…" Roshan said, shining his torch into the abyss, "we're really doing this."

CHAPTER 16

TROUBLE!

Anshuman and Preeti stood outside the entrance, completely at a loss. After a few moments, Preeti broke the silence. "What should we do?"

"Why are you asking me? You're the one who's supposed to know everything!" her brother snapped, clearly annoyed.

"Do I look like an encyclopedia to you?" she retorted. "How am I supposed to know what to do in a situation like this?"

"What do they teach you in school, then?"

"Seriously? The subjects you struggle with, like science and math." she shot back.

The siblings quarreled for a few minutes before sitting down on the ground, exhausted from their banter. After a moment,

Preeti took a deep breath. "Let's start somewhere. We can think our way through this."

Anshuman's eyes brightened. "Do you remember those action movies where the police searched for clues at a crime scene? We can start like that!" he said.

"That sounds like an incredible idea! You're my brother, after all," Preeti chuckled. "Let's split up—I'll search this side, you go over there."

They parted ways, combing the shrine's perimeter. They looked under rocks, climbed trees, and examined the walls for markings or clues. When their efforts yielded nothing, they returned, weary.

"My legs hurt. I feel like a wild animal prowling the woods." Preeti complained, checking her feet for blisters. "Do you have any food? I'm starving."

"I've got a chocolate bar." Anshuman pulled it from his pocket, breaking it in half and offering her a piece. They sat in the dim light of their torches, nibbling on chocolate.

Just as Preeti was about to rise, she froze. "Did you hear that?" she said, swinging her torch around.

"I didn't hear anything," Anshuman replied.

"It sounded like it came from those trees." she said, pointing to a cluster just a few feet away.

They approached the trees and scanned the area for signs of life. After a few minutes of searching, they were about to turn back when Preeti spotted something near the base of the trees. Shining her torch on it, she exclaimed, "It's a cigarette butt! Smells fresh too. Someone must have been here just before us."

"We should keep it, just in case." Anshuman said, carefully picking it up with his handkerchief and tucking it into his pocket.

As they continued their search, Anshuman's torchlight caught several footprints in the soil, leading away from the trees into the woods.

"Preeti, look here!" he called. "There are multiple footprints, and they're all different."

Preeti knelt beside him. "You're right. It looks like there were about five people here, probably having a conversation while one of them smoked."

"Exactly. Do we have anything to copy them?" he asked.

"Yes! I have Rosh's phone. We can take pictures to help identify these people later." She took it out and snapped several photos of the tracks.

Once done, Anshuman suggested, "You should sketch them out for extra precaution."

"I might have some paper and a pen in my backpack." Preeti rummaged through her bag and pulled out a piece of paper. She began sketching the footprints, trying to make each distinct while Anshuman held the light over her.

After she finished, they examined the sketches. "It's not your best work." Anshuman commented, "but better than nothing. You never know when it might come in handy."

Just as they were about to pack up, a rustling noise behind them made them freeze. Footsteps. Somebody was coming towards them.

In a flash, they switched off their torches and crouched behind some bushes. Moments later, someone passed by.

They lay motionless, hardly daring to breathe. As the footsteps faded, they slowly peeked through the bushes.

"I think whoever it was has gone into the courtyard." Preeti whispered as they emerged from their hiding spot.

Suddenly, the phone vibrated in her pocket. She took it out to see an unknown number and answered it.

"YOU HAVE TO GET OUT OF THERE!!!" Arya's frantic voice screamed from the other end.

"What happened, Aaru? Is everything okay?" Preeti asked, panic rising in her chest.

"ALL OF YOU ARE IN DANGER! WARN ROSHAN!" Arya shouted, her voice strained.

"What are you saying? I don't understand...."

Before she could finish, a light flashed behind them. In an instant, Preeti felt a cloth over her nose, and then everything went dark.

CHAPTER 17

TREASURE AT LAST!

Meanwhile, Roshan and the others cautiously made their way through the dark tunnel. It was slippery and musty, and none of them enjoyed it.

"Okay, the tunnel narrows here. Single file, everyone!" Roshan instructed.

As they pressed on, the passage became so low that they had to bend almost double. Hiroshi groaned. "When's this going to end? My back is killing me."

"Same here. I'm so not feeling adventurous right now." Elena grumbled.

"I can't feel my legs!" Nishan exclaimed, exasperated.

"Guys, hang on! We're almost through." Roshan reassured them.

Just then, the passage widened, and the ceiling rose higher. They all sighed in relief, grateful to stand upright. Shining their torches around, they found themselves in what seemed like a room, carved out from the rock. Unlike the damp tunnels, this space felt dry and somewhat comforting.

"This must have been used by soldiers in the past—and now by these lunatics." Roshan thought, illuminating the room with his torch.

At the far end, three tunnels awaited: two leading in opposite directions and one going straight ahead.

"Let's go!" Elena said, stepping forward eagerly.

"Wait!" Roshan interjected. "Do you know which way to go?"

"It's obvious. The one going straight, of course." she replied confidently.

"How do you know that's the right way?" Nishan asked.

"The middle one is always the answer. Duh! Have you never watched a fictional movie?"

"No, Elena. This place might be dangerous. We can't just wander in blindly. Let's check the entrances for any signs that might point us in the right direction." Roshan said firmly.

While the others searched for clues, Roshan wandered to the far corner of the room. Something had caught his eye—a box-like structure. Turning it over, he noticed a lens attached to its side. Suddenly, he realized what it was.

"It's a projector. Probably used to cast the hologram of the shrine." he mused. Beside it was a big drill like object, probably a small part of a bigger contraption. "Probably a part of the object used to generate the shockwaves. Wow, the extent these people can go to in search for a treasure!" he thought to himself.

Just then, Hiroshi called out, "I've found it!"

Everyone gathered at the left tunnel's entrance. Hiroshi pointed his torch at the wall, where an arrow was drawn with chalk, pointing toward the passage.

"Are you sure about that?" Roshan asked, raising a brow.

"I checked. The other two don't have any markings." Hiroshi replied confidently.

"All right then! Left it is!" Roshan declared.

They ventured into the tunnel, which was as dark and musty as the others, with damp spots where water pooled.

Roshan glanced at his watch. Half past three. In a couple of hours, the sun would rise, and Mrs. Watanabe would wake up. "We need to finish this before anyone realizes we're not in bed." he whispered.

As they continued, the narrow passage made them acutely aware of their hunger. Hiroshi pulled out a few slices of cake, sharing them among the group to tide them over.

Suddenly, everyone stopped. Nishan asked, "What's wrong? Is there something ahead?"

"We seem to have reached a dead end. Just a big wall of rock in front of me." Roshan replied.

"Are you sure?" Elena asked, skeptic.

"I'm twelve, not blind. I know what's in front of me." he said, rolling his eyes. Sometimes his friends asked the silliest questions.

He ran his hands over the surface, feeling only layers of bedrock. Then his fingers brushed against a niche cut into the wall. Curiosity piqued, he rummaged inside and found a lever. He tugged on it, and it slid down smoothly.

With a grating sound, a hidden door opened, revealing a magnificent room beyond. They stepped inside, and a dazzling sight greeted them.

The room was crafted from wrought iron, its walls adorned with hundreds of precious stones. Crates and sacks overflowed with golden ingots, while others held rubies, emeralds, and various gems, some as large as eggs.

The awestruck children explored the treasure trove. One box contained a necklace with the largest pearls Elena had ever seen. Another housed a crown made of gold, encrusted with sapphires. A sack lay filled with polished iron swords, their handles studded with semi-precious stones. In one corner stood a samurai armor, crafted from gleaming jade.

"I think I might need to lie down." Nishan said, feeling overwhelmed.

"No wonder they're after this so desperately. This must be worth a fortune!" Roshan said, eyes wide with wonder.

Hiroshi picked up a small sword and pretended to brandish it, making Nishan jump back.

Elena slipped on a gold bracelet bejeweled with diamonds. "Looks good, doesn't it? Preeti would love this!" she admired.

As they marveled at the treasures, a sudden grating sound caught their attention. Horror washed over them as they realized the door was closing on its own!

Hiroshi dashed forward to hold it open, but it shut before he could reach it. *They were trapped*!

CHAPTER 18

TRAPPED!

The four children stood in silence, shocked by what had just happened. The door had slammed shut, leaving them trapped inside.

"Who could've done this?" Elena asked.

"I have no idea. It must've been someone hiding, probably lying in wait for us to walk right into their trap." Roshan replied.

"What should we do?" Nishan asked, his heart pounding.

"What else can we do other than wait?" Roshan said.

As they sat, their hearts racing with fear, the door suddenly slid open. Two men walked in, and the children's mouths fell open as they recognized the first man. It was the archaeologist!

"Happy to see me?" he said, his chuckle sounding sinister.

"What do you want?" Roshan demanded, stepping in front of the others.

"Oh, nothing personal. You see, we mean business, and we don't tolerate meddling in our affairs. You would've been spared if only you'd heeded my advice that day. But don't worry—all of you, including your two dear friends, can enjoy a comfortable stay here." the man said, sounding more like the devil.

Roshan's heart skipped a beat at those words. Preeti and Anshuman!

The man noticed the look on his face and smirked. "Don't worry; they're safe. In fact, they're here right now." He turned toward the door. "Please bring them in!"

Two men entered, dragging in the unconscious children, bound in ropes. Hiroshi looked at one of the men and instantly recognized him, paling in shock.

"KENJI! YOU WERE IN THIS THE ENTIRE TIME?!" he shouted. "All those months of working in our home, it was all just a cover-up!"

"Shut up, you little pest!" the grim man shouted back, shocking the children even more.

"So you can speak quite well, huh? You really are a piece of work!" Roshan said, angry at himself for not discovering the truth sooner.

"One more word from any of you, and your bodies will be full of holes!" the man growled, brandishing a revolver.

"What are you going to do with us?" Roshan asked the archeologist.

"Nothing. We'll just make sure you stay here and keep your mouths shut until we conclude our business. Once we've collected all the treasure, we'll be off, and you will be on your own."

The men laughed menacingly.

"Let us go! You won't get anything by keeping us here!" Elena shouted at the retreating men, anxiety creeping in.

The men merely let out evil chuckles as they left, closing the entrance behind them.

Everyone gathered around the two children, who were beginning to stir.

Seeing themselves bound tightly, Preeti asked, puzzled and dizzy, "What happened? Why are we tied up? Where are we?"

"In a minute, Prits. You'll know everything soon." Roshan said as he untied her.

A few minutes later, they were sitting on the crates, sharing their experiences. When Roshan reached the part about Kenji's true self, Preeti exclaimed, "I always knew something was off about that man!"

"Well, your suspicions were right. Kenji is with those men, and now he's trapped all of us here...for good!" Nishan said, glancing anxiously at the entrance.

CHAPTER 19

HANA TO THE RESCUE

The children sat in silence, completely clueless. They had nothing to eat or tell the time, as the men had taken their bags, watches, and even Roshan's phone. They huddled in the dim room, hoping the men would return—even if it was only to collect the treasure.

"I wish we could call someone." Elena said after a while. "I really want to get out of here."

"Yeah, if only we had the phone." Preeti sighed sadly.

Roshan placed a comforting hand on her shoulder. "I know you're feeling scared and lost right now, but have faith.

Everything will be alright." he said, trying to sound more composed than he felt.

"I'm hungry. It feels like there are rats doing the salsa in my stomach." Nishan grumbled, and his comment drew giggles that lightened the mood for a moment.

As they sat there, feeling despondent, Roshan heard a noise that resembled a cat scratching at a door, seemingly coming from outside. He signaled the others to listen, and everyone perked up their ears. Soon, they heard the grating sound of a door sliding open. Turning, they saw the silhouette of a small figure in the doorway... Hana!

She grinned as the children stared at her in disbelief.

"Hana, is that really you?" Nishan asked, finally finding his voice. "Have you been following us?"

The girl nodded, momentarily awestruck by the treasures surrounding her.

"Oh, so that must be the rustling I heard out there." Preeti thought to herself.

"You cheeky little monkey!" Roshan exclaimed, ruffling her hair. "Did any of the bad men see you?"

She shook her head.

"They've probably gone off to arrange transport for the treasure." Roshan said, glancing around the room. "Now's our chance. Let's make a dash for it!"

As everyone escaped from the vault, Elena hesitated at the threshold, then turned back to grab a few golden ingots and jewels, stuffing them into her pockets.

"Just in case." she said, rejoining the group as they closed the entrance behind them.

They retraced their steps, careful not to lose their footing in the dark. Hana led the way, as sure-footed as a mountain goat. Roshan marveled at her ability to navigate the pitch black.

Half running, half crawling, they reached the spacious room at the tunnel's entrance. Just as they paused to catch their breath, they heard footsteps approaching.

"They're back!" Roshan whispered, grabbing Hana and pushing her into the shadows. "QUICK! EVERYBODY HIDE!"

CHAPTER 20

THE ADVENTURE ENDS

As the footsteps drew closer, the children slinked into the shadows. Just as they hid, the men passed by, their voices and footsteps revealing that there were three of them, headed straight for the vault, Kenji among them.

Once they were out of earshot, Roshan emerged from hiding. "They're gone! Now's our chance to escape. Let's get out before they realize we're missing!"

As everyone ran out, Hana slipped away to follow the men, a plan forming in her mind—one that would allow her to get back at them.

She stealthily observed as they opened the door and entered. Soon, Kenji's angry voice echoed through the room. "Where are the kids?! Who set them free?"

Seizing the opportunity, Hana dashed forward and pulled the lever on the wall. Before the men could grasp what was happening, the entrance slammed shut behind them.

Hana nearly burst into laughter at the sound of their frantic screams and pounding on the door. She smirked, as if to say, "This is what you get for trying to harm my friends!" and quickly ran off to join the others.

Meanwhile, the rest of the group had reached the large opening in the rock. Thankfully, the men had left it open.

The sun shone brightly on the horizon as the children emerged, and they had to pause for a moment to adjust to the light, after having spent so long in the darkness.

As they basked in the sun, police sirens suddenly blared in the distance. Roshan smiled. "Good job, Aaru." he muttered under his breath.

A few minutes later, the children sat in the living room, sipping hot cups of green tea while recounting their adventure to the Senior Inspector, who was taking notes. Preeti handed him the sketches she had made, and Anshuman showed him the cigarette butt he'd found. Elena placed the jewels on the table, leaving the policeman amazed.

"I must say, you kids are incredibly brave to have gone through all that. You've made it much easier for us to catch the remaining culprits." he said.

"Do you know who these men are, sir?" Roshan asked.

The Inspector replied, "They're part of a black market ring with connections worldwide. They steal historically significant objects and sell them abroad as forgeries at ridiculously low prices."

The children exchanged looks of disbelief. An object dating back hundreds of years, worth millions, sold for just a few hundred as a fake! These men were truly criminals.

Mrs. Watanabe entered the room with bowls of steaming hot noodles, overhearing the conversation. "I never expected Kenji to be involved in this. That explains why he suddenly showed up at our door a year ago, asking for a job. He must have been scouting out plans right under our noses!" She let out a heavy sigh of relief. She had been very baffled when Arya and Fumiko had woken her up in the middle of the night, screeching about the others trapped in the shrine. Worried about the children's safety, she had called the police.

The Inspector stood to leave. "I must go now. We need to send men into the vault to retrieve the treasure and arrest the three men trapped there. As for the other two, it won't be long before they're behind bars too, thanks to you kids."

He turned to the children. "Great work, everyone. Our countries need young people like you. I'm sure you'll grow up to be great detectives."

Everyone smiled at his words.

After he left, the children trudged upstairs, too exhausted to wash up or even change, and fell asleep as soon as their heads hit the pillows.

The next day, as they sat down for breakfast, the old woman burst through the door, Hana by her side, beaming with joy.

"What happened? Why do you look so happy?" Mrs. Watanabe asked.

The old woman replied, ecstatic, "The police arrested the men! They were so exhausted from being locked in the vault that they gave up without a fight. By this evening, the police will return all the belongings the men seized from the children. As for the treasure, it will be moved to a different location under strict surveillance."

Everyone heaved a sigh of relief. Finally, everything was back to normal.

"This has been quite the adventure." Elena said. "I'll never forget it."

"Me neither." said Roshan. "Now we just have to wait for Dad and Mr. Watanabe to come back so we can share our story with them."

"And shop!" Arya chimed in. "Remember, we agreed to go shopping before heading home. I really want to buy a bell for Biscuit's collar. It'll look so cute!"

"And who's going to pay for that?" Nishan asked, raising an eyebrow.

"Why, it's obviously going to be you." she said, giggling mischievously.

"Why am I not surprised?" Nishan said and rolled his eyes, and everyone burst into laughter.

THE END